TALL TALE

TALL TALE

The Unbelievable Adventures of Pecos Bill

A Novel by Todd Strasser
Based on the Motion Picture from Walt Disney Pictures
In association with Caravan Pictures
Executive Producer Bill Badalato
Based on the Screenplay Written by Steven L. Bloom & Robert Rodat
Produced by Joe Roth and Roger Birnbaum
Directed by Jeremiah Chechik

Disney
PRESS
NEW YORK

To Meghan and Lauren,
Happy trails to you!

Darn you, Samson, c'mon!"
In the middle of a broad dirt pasture, Daniel Hackett, age
twelve, stood nose to nose with a stubborn brown horse.

"I said, 'C'mon!'" Daniel grabbed the leather reins
and pulled as hard as he could, but the horse wouldn't
budge. Behind Samson was a plow, which the horse had
clearly lost interest in pulling.

Daniel threw down the reins in disgust and pushed
the hair out of his eyes. He looked out across the pasture
at the endless straight furrows that he and Samson had
plowed over the past few days. Beyond the pasture was
his family's one-story wooden farmhouse, and behind
that was the wide, tree-lined Paradise River. Beyond the
river were the snowcapped mountains and the broad
blue sky.

Daniel and his folks lived in Paradise Valley, and Daniel imagined it was about as far away from civilization
as one could get in 1905.

Daniel hated living in Paradise Valley and wished he could be anyplace but there. He turned back to the horse.

"You know how much trouble you're getting me into?" he shouted angrily. "If I don't get the other half of this pasture plowed by tonight, Pa will tan my hide."

But the horse wouldn't budge. In a way, Daniel was relieved. What he hated even more than living in Paradise Valley was working on the farm. Daniel liked to think that there was a whole world out there for him. A world beyond the mountains. Away from the farm. Places he'd read about in magazines. Places where people didn't have to work behind a plow from dawn to dusk.

Samson's ears suddenly flicked forward. Daniel knew that the horse had heard something. Daniel listened, too, and detected a distant puttering. On the narrow dirt road that ran along the edge of the pasture, a motorized contraption was rolling past, kicking up a plume of dust.

Daniel could hardly believe his eyes. *A horseless carriage!* Daniel had never seen an automobile except in a magazine. He ran across the field to get a better look, but by the time he got to the road the buggy had rounded the bend, leaving nothing but dust in its wake.

It must be headed into town, Daniel thought. Overcome with curiosity, Daniel left Samson in the middle of the pasture and took a shortcut to town.

The automobile was parked in front of the sheriff's office. It was painted yellow and was trimmed in the shiniest chrome Daniel had ever seen. Wisps of steam were still rising from its radiator. It reminded Daniel of a beautiful animal, sleek and powerful. Daniel ran over to it and jumped up on the running board. He ran his hand over the wooden steering wheel and the glass dials. The engine was purring low, and the fragrant smell of the polished black leather seats was as sweet as anything Daniel could imagine.

"Hey, get offa there!"

Startled, Daniel jumped back. A mean, hard-looking man with a pockmarked face and a black derby was looking down at him. Beside him was Sheriff Peters, puffing on a huge cigar.

"Darn hicks got no respect for private property," the stranger in the derby grumbled. He turned away from Daniel and back to Sheriff Peters. "Now, remember," he warned him, "Mr. Stiles wants the rest of the deeds by tonight."

"You tell Mr. Stiles they're farmers, not fighters," Sheriff Peters replied. "A little gentle persuasion, and they'll sell like the sheep they are."

Daniel was too intrigued with the buggy to pay much attention to what the men said.

"Mr. Stiles don't like trouble," the stranger said.

"A few may squawk some," Sheriff Peters said. He eyed Daniel. "But when push comes to shove, they'll fold."

"They'd better." The stranger spit on the ground, climbed into the buggy, and drove off. Daniel watched longingly as the contraption puttered out of town, kicking up a plume of dust.

Maybe someday I'll drive a horseless carriage, he thought. He sighed.

Suddenly Daniel had a sickening thought. He groaned miserably. Samson!

TWO

Daniel ran all the way back home from town, but he was too late. The north pasture was a mess. Without anyone to guide him, Samson had wandered the pasture aimlessly, pulling the plow every which way. All Daniel's work was ruined.

Now, he knew, there'd be hell to pay.

Daniel found his father in the barn rubbing salve into Samson's forelegs. Jonas Hackett wasn't a big man, but he was muscular and strong. And he had a temper to match. He stared up angrily at Daniel, then looked back down.

Daniel nervously scraped his toe on the hard dirt floor. "Sorry, Pa," he said.

"Sorry just ain't good enough," his father muttered. "You're darn lucky Samson didn't break a leg."

"But there was a horseless carriage," Daniel said excitedly. "Right here in Paradise Valley! Just like in the magazine!"

"A horseless carriage, you say?" His father squinted up at him.

Daniel nodded.

Jonas sighed and shook his head. "I knew they was coming. I was just hoping it'd be later rather than sooner." He looked at his son. "Is that why you left your work undone? To chase after some darn machine?"

Daniel tried to explain. "But Pa! It's the transportation of tomorrow! Only it's here today!"

"Today," his father snapped angrily, "you were supposed to finish plowing the north pasture."

"But Pa . . ."

"But Pa nothing! This is a farm, Daniel. Work's got to be done when it's supposed to be done!"

"I hate this farm," Daniel grumbled to himself.

"What'd you say?" his father asked, raising an eyebrow.

All the resentment that had been building up inside of Daniel suddenly burst out. "I said I hate this farm! I wish you'd sell it!"

"You don't know what you're saying," his father said.

"I sure do!" Daniel yelled. "This farm's nothing! It's just a dried-up, miserable piece of ground!"

"Hold your tongue," his father warned him. Jonas rose to his feet and pointed. "There's wood to be split. Get to it!"

But Daniel was too angry to keep silent. "Someday," he promised his father, "I'm gonna get me a horseless carriage! And I'm going to drive right out of Paradise Valley and I ain't never coming back!"

Daniel turned angrily and came face-to-face with his mother. She was a small woman with blue eyes and wheat-colored hair. She was holding Eli, Daniel's four-month-old brother. It was obvious from her expression that she'd heard every word.

"A man works and slaves to give his son something worth having," his father complained from behind him, "and he throws it back like it don't mean beans!"

"Go out and split the wood," his mother told Daniel gently. Daniel knew better than to argue with her.

As he trudged out of the barn, he could hear his folks quarreling. "Shoot," Daniel muttered to himself. If his father had his way, Daniel knew he'd be trapped on this dusty patch of earth for the rest of his life. Why couldn't his father understand that farming was *his* dream, not Daniel's?

He spent the rest of the afternoon splitting wood. The sun was low and beginning to turn orange when his father came around to the woodpile, carrying two fishing poles.

"Sun will be setting soon," he said. "Trout must be near starving. Let's go get us some dinner."

"I got chores," Daniel replied coldly.

"They can keep," his father said. "The fish can't."

———

A little while later, Daniel and his father were sitting in a rowboat anchored in the Paradise River. The wispy clouds had turned pink and amber.

"Right nice sunset, huh?" his father said.

"I reckon," Daniel replied dully.

"Some folks say sunrise is the prettiest part of the day. Me, I'll take a good sunset. Work's done, and a man's got time to appreciate what's around him."

"I reckon," Daniel muttered again. There was nothing around him that he particularly appreciated.

They fished in silence for a while, then his father said, "Did I ever tell you about the time Pecos Bill wrestled John Henry at Upside-Down Mountain?"

"About a hundred times," Daniel said.

"That many, huh?" his father replied with a hint of a smile. "What about the morning Pecos spiked Paul Bunyan's flapjacks with hot chili peppers?"

"Paul Bunyan's breath came spurting out like fire and burned down the entire Arizona Territory," Daniel said, reciting from memory.

"I reckon I told you that one, too. How about the time old Pecos took on single-handed fifty of the toughest, meanest outlaws this side of the Rockies?"

"No," Daniel answered irritably, "because it never happened. C'mon, Pa, I ain't a kid no more."

"Is that a fact?" Jonas asked.

"A person would have to be a fool to take on fifty men," Daniel suggested.

"Well," countered Jonas, "sometimes the smart thing to do ain't the right thing to do. At least that's how Pecos Bill figured it. Besides, Pecos was never one to back down from a fight. And seeing that there were only fifty of them, he wasn't too worried."

Daniel made a big gesture of rolling his eyes.

"Them fifty varmints slapped leather," Jonas said. "Pecos emptied both six-guns and shot off the trigger fingers of every one."

"How did he shoot off fifty trigger fingers with only twelve bullets?" Daniel asked.

"Easy," his father replied. "He just lined up the shots so he got four or five fingers with each bullet."

"That's impossible," Daniel insisted, "and you know it."

"Nothing's impossible if you believe hard enough."

"It's just a tall tale," Daniel said.

"That don't mean it ain't true."

"Crazy talk," Daniel grumbled.

"Then Pecos swung his lariat and roped a passing twister," his father continued. "He rode it off into the sky."

"Pecos Bill ain't real," Daniel said flatly.

"Sure he is."

"Then where is he?"

"Out there," Jonas said with a broad sweep of his hand. "Out where there's still enough room for a man to wander. And where the land is still young and wild."

Daniel shook his head resignedly. When he was young, Daniel had enjoyed his father's stories. But he was older now.

His father put his hand over his heart. "I swear by the Code of the West," he intoned solemnly, "that Pecos Bill is as real as you and me. You ain't forgot the Code, have you?"

"No, Pa."

"Respect the land," recited his father. "Defend the defenseless. And don't never spit in front of women and children."

"Sure, Pa." Daniel let out a big sigh.

● THREE ●

That night Daniel sat in his room flipping through a magazine. He was looking at a photograph of the Brooklyn Bridge in New York City. His parents were in the next room arguing.

"What do you want me to do, Sarah?" his father asked. "Bow down like the rest of them and sell my land?"

"If it means staying alive, yes," answered his mother. "I've heard about Stiles. He's mean and vicious, and he plans to own all of Paradise Valley by the time the tunnel's done."

Daniel remembered the stranger in town saying something about a Mr. Stiles that afternoon.

"I can't allow that," Jonas said. "We've worked too hard."

"Why do you always have to be the hero, Jonas? Why are you always the one who sticks his neck out?"

There was a brief pause. "Somebody's got to," his father said firmly.

Daniel heard a chair scraping along the floor. He pushed open his door a crack just in time to see his father take his hunting rifle from the mantel.

"No guns, Jonas," his mother pleaded. "This isn't one of those stories you tell Daniel. Why are you so quick to risk your life? What about your family? What about us?"

"That's why I'm going," Jonas said. He put his arm around his wife's shoulders and hugged her. "I'll be back before you know it."

"Please be careful," she said.

Jonas opened the front door and stepped out into the night.

Daniel was frightened. He had never seen his father take his rifle anywhere but to hunt. Where could he be going? he wondered. If there was trouble, maybe his father would need help. Closing his door, Daniel pulled on his jacket and climbed out the window.

A little while later Daniel slipped in through the back door of the Paradise Valley Church. The pews were filled with farmers. Daniel recognized most of them. Like his father, they were honest, hardworking men. Daniel climbed the stairs to the choir loft, where he could watch and listen without being seen.

Daniel listened to the men talk.

"What's Stiles want with Paradise Valley, anyway?" one of them asked.

"He wants what's in the ground," said Daniel's father

ominously. "Iron," Jonas said, "and coal, copper, and oil, too."

"Well, what's he plan to do with them once he's got them?" a third farmer asked.

"He's building a railroad tunnel through the mountain. Once it's done, he'll bring trains in here and haul everything out."

"Are you saying this Stiles feller is building this tunnel by himself?"

"No sir," said Jonas. "He's got a bunch of rich Eastern fellers backing him. They put up the money, and he puts up the muscle."

"Well then," said a farmer named Bronson, "I guess I'm selling. I remember Stiles when he was a gunslinger. He wasn't a man who took no for an answer."

"I say he can't make us sell," Jonas countered. "Not if we all stick together!"

Just then the doors at the back of the church were flung open. The crowd fell silent as a tall man came sauntering down the aisle. He was wearing an expensive black suit, and two pearl-handled pistols were slung low on his hips. A long scar ran down his cheek under his left eye.

The man stepped up to the pulpit and turned to the crowd.

"My name is Stiles," he said, "and my pa was a farmer. I know what it's like to work the land until your hands are blistered and raw." His eyes swung slowly from side to side. "I know what it's like to break your back day in and day out, fighting to scratch out a living, praying that the crop will come in, hanging on when it don't."

Some of the farmers nodded in agreement.

"I got out," Stiles said, his voice climbing. "I saw my chance and I took it! Now I'm offering you a way out."

Stiles smiled and suddenly held up a fistful of bills. "Fifty dollars an acre!"

An excited chorus of murmurs broke out among the farmers.

"Cold cash!" Stiles said, waving the money like a flag. "With this kind of money you can buy yourself a new house in town. You could have a Victrola, indoor plumbing, electricity."

The farmers rustled with excitement, but none more than Daniel. Imagine, he thought excitedly, a room lit with electric lights instead of lanterns.

"What if we don't want those things?" someone inquired. Daniel did not even have to look to see who it was. He recognized the voice. It was his father's.

"You'll want those things," Stiles answered. "The whole country wants them. That's what makes America what it is! Factories going around the clock. Oil wells. Steel mills to make steel for buildings. Cities! That's the future!"

Jonas stared at Stiles, unmoved.

"But supposing you're against progress," Stiles said, addressing not Jonas but the crowd. "Supposing you want to hold back the clock and waste the rest of your days sweating behind a plow. Well, for the fifty dollars an acre you'll get here, you can go over to Jefferson County and buy six times as much land."

"It's a no-lose proposition," one farmer said. There was scattered agreement among the farmers.

"In a pig's eye it is!" Jonas objected angrily.

Daniel winced. Why did his father always have to be the one to fight progress?

There was an awkward silence as Stiles stared down at Jonas from the pulpit. "And who might you be, friend?" he asked finally, twisting his lips into a smile.

"The name's Jonas Hackett," he said. "And you ain't no friend of mine."

The smile disappeared from Stiles's face. Daniel was horrified as he watched his father turn to the crowd.

"What happens after Mr. Stiles and his partners from the East are all done ripping and tearing apart Paradise Valley like they did over the mountain in Gravity Valley?" he asked. "You don't think Jefferson County will be next?

"Pete," he said, appealing to a farmer on his right, "you're from West Virginia. You know what it's like to see your land ripped up for mines." He turned to his left. "Barney, you came here from Texas, like me. You saw how they ruined the land with oil wells. Just about every person in this room left their homes and families to escape exactly what Mr. Stiles is proposing to do right here."

"That's enough, Hackett," Stiles said. "I warn you, I don't abide troublemakers."

Jonas ignored the threat. "How many times can a man

pull up stakes?" he asked them. "How many times can he plant new roots? You give in now, and you know where you'll end up? Working in one of Mr. Stiles's factories twelve hours a day, six days a week!"

"But Jonas," a farmer said. "He's offering fifty dollars an acre."

"That's a lot of money," Jonas conceded. "No question about it."

"You're darned right it is," Stiles agreed. "Enough money to buy just about anything you ever dreamed of."

"Everything except what we already have," Jonas shot back. "Room to grow. Air you can breathe. Neighbors who care."

Jonas pulled a piece of paper from his pocket and waved it in the air.

"This is the deed to my farm," he said. "It's got my blood and sweat on it. It's where my children were born and where I want to be buried. I don't know about you, but that's worth a lot more than fifty dollars an acre. To me, it's worth more than any price."

Daniel was astonished when the farmers around the room began to nod their heads in agreement. Were they crazy? he wondered.

"You can't stand in the way of progress, Mr. Hackett!" shouted Stiles. "The tunnel will be finished. Industry will come. It's industry that has made this country great."

"It seems to me that it's the land and people who made this country great," Jonas said. "I ain't saying I'm against progress, but I sure do have a problem with blind greed." He looked at Stiles hard, eye to eye. "I ain't selling."

The farmers burst into thunderous applause. Daniel couldn't believe it. They were all congratulating Jonas and slapping him on the back. His father had won!

Daniel scampered down the stairs and exited the church through a side door into an alley. He didn't want his father to get home first and discover that he had sneaked out. He had gotten himself into enough trouble today. He was just about to turn the corner of the alley when someone jumped in front of him.

"Daniel!" his father snapped. "What in blazes are you doing here?"

"I heard you and Ma arguing and I got worried," Daniel explained. "Why can't we sell, Pa?"

"Quiet! Listen to me!" His father tucked the deed to the farm into the pocket of Daniel's jacket. "Take this," he said, "and don't let no one have it, no matter what."

"But Pa—"

"No matter what," his father repeated. "Understand, Daniel?"

Daniel nodded.

"Now go!"

Daniel hesitated. He didn't want to leave his father. Suddenly Stiles and his gang of toughs appeared at the entrance to the alley. They were all carrying guns.

Daniel was frozen with fear.

"Go, blast you!" his father shouted.

Daniel ran as fast as he could.

Bang! A single gunshot rang out, shattering the stillness. Daniel skidded to a stop and looked back. His heart was pounding, and tears were running down his face.

"Pa!"

●FOUR●

Daniel stared blankly into the fire. He had been up all night and day, but he felt more numb than tired. Three of his father's friends sat in a corner, talking quietly. Daniel's mother, her eyes red and puffy, stood at the sideboard slicing bread. Eli cooed in his crib.

The door to the bedroom opened, and Doc Perkins stepped out. Sarah Hackett stepped anxiously toward him.

"I've done everything I can do," he said. "It's in the Lord's hands now."

Through the open door, Daniel caught a glimpse of his father lying motionless in the bed. His shoulder was heavily bandaged.

"I'm selling," announced one of the farmers. He looked toward Jonas, then shook his head. "No piece of ground is worth dying for."

Dying? Daniel thought.

Suddenly Daniel jumped up and ran out the door. It was as if somehow he thought he could outrun the fear. He ran all the way to the river. He remembered the lazy afternoon he and his father had shared only yesterday. *Now his father was going to die.* He climbed down into the rowboat and lay down. He tried to forget. But he couldn't. Daniel cried until he fell asleep.

It was hot when he awoke, almost as if he were lying next to a bonfire. The sun was a huge flat disk in the sky, and buzzards circled high overhead. Daniel blinked into the blinding sunlight. He was lying in the boat, and three black vultures perched on the gunwale, staring at him hungrily.

"He sure looks dead to me," a raspy voice said.

Daniel sat up and looked around. The rowboat was stranded in the middle of an enormous dried-up lake bed.

What's more, standing beside the boat were three of the dirtiest, mangiest, most disgusting prospectors Daniel had ever seen.

"Where am I?" Daniel asked. "Who are you?"

Startled, the three mangy prospectors quickly drew their guns.

"Stick 'em up!" one of them said, pointing his gun in Daniel's face.

"But—," Daniel protested.

"Hands over yer head!" shouted another. "Now!"

Daniel raised his hands over his head. One of the prospectors stepped into the boat, yanked Daniel to his feet, and began to search him. He pulled the deed and some change out of Daniel's pockets. .

"That's mine!" Daniel cried, grabbing for the deed. "Give it back!"

But he pushed Daniel away and turned to his buddies. "Sixteen cents! Hot spit!"

"Any gold in his teeth?" one of them asked.

The prospector grabbed Daniel by the neck and pried open his mouth. "Two . . . three . . . four fillings."

"Tsk, tsk," said the third man. He shook his head and leered. "Someone ain't been brushing after every meal."

The men burst out laughing.

"Grub, let me kill this one," said the one named Jeb. "You killed the last two in a row."

"That's because I'm better at it than you," replied Grub.

"C'mon, fair's fair," whined Jeb.

"Oh, all right."

Twitching with anticipation, Jeb pointed his pistol at Daniel. "So long, kid. Sorry to stunt your growth."

Bang! A shot rang out, and Jeb clutched his hand and howled in pain.

"Somebody done shot off my trigger finger!" he cried.

They spun around to see who'd fired the shot, but all they saw was rippling waves of heat rising up from the desert. Then, far in the distance, a small dust funnel appeared, and out of the funnel came a tiny speck. It was coming closer.

Daniel's jaw dropped. It was a cowboy on horseback!

The third prospector, Zeb, reached for his rifle.

Bang! Another shot rang out that knocked Zeb's hat clear off his head. Zeb quickly raised his hands in surrender.

The cowboy was riding toward them on a magnificent chestnut stallion, reins free, sighting down the barrel of a rifle.

Grub reached for his pistol.

Bang! The cowboy fired again. This time the buckle on Grub's gun belt shattered, and his guns dropped to the ground. Daniel couldn't believe it.

The three prospectors tried to run away, but the cowboy swung his lariat over his head in a wide circle and threw it, lassoing them to a halt.

Daniel stared in wonder as the cowboy nonchalantly dismounted. He was covered from head to toe with dust, and his chin was unshaven. He was wearing a tall gray hat, what might at one time have been a blue-striped shirt, and leather chaps.

"Good boy, Widowmaker!" The cowboy patted his horse and turned to Daniel. "You okay, kid?"

"I . . . I think so," Daniel said.

"Ahhhhhhh!" screamed one of the prospectors. Daniel couldn't believe his eyes. The rope the cowboy had used to lasso the three prospectors was really a rattlesnake!

"It's okay, Slim," the cowboy said to the snake. Daniel watched the rattler slither away from the three men and crawl up the horse's leg into a saddlebag.

"Who are you?" Daniel asked.

"I'm a ring-tailed roarer!" the cowboy boasted. "I can

draw faster, shoot straighter, and ride harder than any man alive! I ride cyclones and—"

"Excuse me," interrupted Daniel, "but you have a name, don't you?"

"I was just getting to that," the cowboy replied. "I'm the ripsnortingest cowboy who ever rode north, south, east, or west of the Rio Grande. I'm Pecos Bill!"

"Sure," Daniel smirked, "and I'm Santy Claus."

The cowboy frowned and turned to his horse. "Friendly cuss, ain't he, Widowmaker?"

The horse snorted and glowered at Daniel.

"The name's Daniel Hackett," he said.

The cowboy stuck out a weathered hand, and Daniel shook it. His grip was like iron.

"Daniel," the cowboy said, turning his Winchester on the three mangy prospectors. "I believe these varmints have something that belongs to you."

Daniel retrieved the deed to the farm and his sixteen cents. Meanwhile, the three sorry prospectors fell to their knees and begged Pecos Bill to have mercy on them.

"C'mon, mister, let us go," Grub pleaded. "We was only fooling."

"We wasn't gonna make the boy suffer," said Zeb with a sniff.

"Yeah," added Jeb. "One shot, and that would have been it. He wouldn't have felt a thing."

"I should probably plug you three right now," Pecos said sternly. "But I make it a rule never to kill a man on Sunday."

"But it's Wednesday," Zeb said.

"Shut up, you fool!" Grub snapped.

"Wednesday?" Pecos looked surprised. Then he smiled and reached for his pistols. The three prospectors scrambled to their feet and hightailed it across the desert.

Bang! Bang! Bang! The cowboy fired into the air, and the men screamed and ran even faster. Daniel watched the cowboy curiously.

"Who are you really?" he asked.

"I told you."

"Mister, you're crazy," Daniel said. "Pecos Bill ain't real. Everybody knows that."

"Is that any way to thank a man for saving your skin?" he asked, twirling his guns so fast they were just a blur. "What brings you to Texas anyway, Daniel?"

"Texas?" Daniel repeated in surprise. "Is that where I am?"

"Where'd you think you was?" Pecos asked.

Daniel told him that the last thing he remembered, he was falling asleep in the boat back in Paradise Valley.

"You floated all the way down here from Paradise Valley?" the cowboy asked.

"I can't explain it neither," Daniel said. "But it's the truth."

Pecos started to climb back onto his horse.

"Wait, where're you going?" Daniel asked.

"South, down Mexico way."

"South?" Daniel gasped. "But I've got to get back home.

My pa's hurt bad. I got to take care of my ma and my little brother."

"That may be," Pecos replied. "But if you stay out here, you're bound to fry faster than a bug on a hot skillet. You'd best come with me."

He reached down and pulled Daniel up behind him on the horse, and they started off across the seemingly endless expanse of desert.

Daniel wasn't happy about heading south, but he had to concede that he owed this cowboy his life.

"Listen . . . whoever you are. Thanks."

"Just living up to the Code," he drawled.

"The Code of the West?" Daniel asked.

The cowboy took off his hat, spit on the ground, and put it back on.

This has to be a joke, Daniel thought to himself.

•FIVE•

After riding for hours through nothing but desert, they finally came upon a small wooded glade beside a waterfall.

"Good boy, Widowmaker," Daniel said, patting the horse's side as he dismounted. Suddenly the horse reared up angrily. Daniel stumbled backward and fell to the ground.

"Whoa, boy," Pecos called to the horse. "Settle down." He turned to Daniel. "Widowmaker's kind of particular about folks taking liberties with him," the cowboy explained in hushed tones. "Last feller who tried that, Widowmaker kicked him so hard he ended halfway to the moon. He bounced up and down for a month of Sundays. Finally I had to shoot him down so he could have a proper burial. That's how Widowmaker got his name, on account of leaving the feller's wife less a husband."

Daniel frowned. "The moon's thousands of miles away," he said. "No way a man could bounce that high."

"You sure do know a lot," Pecos said. "So how's this for plain English? Stay away from the horse or he'll kill you."

They settled in for the evening and had some dinner. As they sat facing the campfire, Daniel told Pecos the story of how Stiles and his men had shot his father in an attempt to get the deed.

"And now Pa could die just because he wanted to hold on to a piece of ground," Daniel said bitterly. "If I hadn't promised Pa to take care of the deed, I'd give the darn thing away."

"Is that a fact?" Pecos raised his eyebrows.

"Ma warned him not to stand up to Stiles," Daniel said. "But Pa had to go be a hero."

"Seems like there's no room for heroes no more," the cowboy said.

Behind them, Widowmaker neighed impatiently as if he wanted to have a word with the cowboy. Pecos got up and walked over. Immediately they fell into a heated discussion. Daniel could only make out bits and pieces of it, but it seemed to have something to do with a filly down in Mexico.

"I know I promised," the cowboy explained wearily to the horse. "And I'll make good on it . . . someday."

After a time, the cowboy came back to the fire and crawled into his bedroll. Daniel was tempted to ask him what the argument was about. But first Daniel would have to figure out how a man could argue with a horse. It was crazy!

He crawled deeper into his bedroll and soon felt his eyelids growing heavy. He was just about to fall asleep when a terrible roar pierced the night.

Ahhhhhhhwwwwooooooooo!

Daniel sat up straight and stared wildly into the dark. "What was *that*?" he asked.

"Cliffside grounder," the cowboy replied with a yawn. "Been a long time since I heard one."

"What's a cliffside grounder?" Daniel asked.

"Good question," he answered. "Some say it's like a buffalo, only with the teeth of a mountain lion. Others say it's more like a grizzly with the horns of an elk. Whatever it is, it's one fearsome critter."

"What do you mean, 'Some say'?" Daniel asked.

"Far as I know, no one's ever set eyes on one and lived to tell about it."

"There ain't no such thing," Daniel said stubbornly. "There can't be."

"That's what you said about me," replied Pecos. Then he rolled over and went to sleep.

The next morning Daniel awoke to a surprise. Where the wooded glade had been the night before, now there was a field of yellow and red and blue wildflowers as far as the eye could see. As Daniel started to rise, the flowers suddenly took flight. The flowers were butterflies—thousands of them!

"Kind of makes it all worthwhile, don't it?" said the cowboy as he hitched his saddle to Widowmaker.

Daniel, however, had more important matters on his mind than butterflies and flowers.

"I ain't going to Mexico," Daniel said.

The cowboy turned to Daniel and smiled. "Who said anything about Mexico? We're heading north."

"To Paradise Valley?" Daniel asked, surprised.

Pecos nodded. "Got some business to settle."

"Why go out of your way for me?" Daniel asked.

"I got my reasons," Pecos replied mysteriously. "Now, you coming or ain't you?"

"Listen, mister," Daniel said.

"Name's Pecos."

"Okay, Pecos," Daniel said. "All I want is to get back to Paradise Valley. I'm not looking for a fight with Stiles."

"Sometimes the fight comes looking for you."

"But Stiles has a lot of men," Daniel protested. "It'd be a hundred to one. You can't win against those odds."

"Odds are like a sheepman's socks," Pecos replied. "When they stink, change them."

Later that day they rode into a forest of redwoods so thick and tall they blocked out the sun.

"Makes me think of Paul," Pecos said. "Last time I saw him was—"

"Paul who?" Daniel interrupted.

"Paul Bunyan."

"Yeah, right." Daniel smirked.

The cowboy glared at Daniel over his shoulder. "To go on with the story I was telling before I was so rudely interrupted," he said, "last time I saw Paul was just after the winter of the blue snow."

"There's no such thing as blue snow," Daniel said.

"It was the coldest winter the world had ever known," he said, ignoring Daniel. "Paul had found a baby ox bobbing up and down in a big block of ice in the Great Lakes."

"And he was blue, right?" Daniel asked.

"Blue as a robin's egg. Paul named him Babe, and they been together ever since. Whoa!" The cowboy pulled the reins on Widowmaker. What had been a lush forest was now nothing but a sea of splintered tree branches and stumps.

"Looks like Paul's been here," Daniel said.

"This ain't Paul's way," the cowboy said soberly. "Something tells me we've wandered into the wrong pond."

They continued riding and soon came upon a huge machine on enormous metal wheels that was cutting down a dozen trees at a time. Teams of loggers trimmed off the branches, then rolled the stripped trunks down a log flume to a river below.

They followed the trail of logs downriver to a logging camp. A sign read Stiles Logging Co. They stopped beside a sawmill, where a long conveyor belt was feeding logs continuously into a giant buzz saw. The cowboy jumped off Widowmaker and climbed a flight of stairs into the noisy sawmill house. Daniel followed him up to a second-floor catwalk and heard him ask a group of plaid-shirted loggers if they'd seen any sign of Paul Bunyan.

"Never heard of him," one of the loggers yelled over the screeching of the mechanical saws.

"That's because he don't exist!" Daniel said.

The cowboy shot Daniel a reproving look, then turned back to the loggers. "You sure you never heard of Paul Bunyan, the greatest logger of them all?"

The loggers shook their heads and pushed past him on their way down the catwalk.

The cowboy had just turned to leave when an old man pushing a broom stopped him. The old man motioned the cowboy and Daniel into a room and hastily pulled down the blinds.

"You looking for Big Paul?" he asked.

"You know him?" Pecos turned and gave Daniel a triumphant look.

"Know him?" The old man grinned. "By cracky, I flipped more flapjacks, slung more hash, and baked more biscuits trying to fill that belly! Never could, neither."

"He knows Paul, all right." Pecos smiled.

"Paul pulled up stakes when the first machinery moved in," the old man said. "I heard he settled in the great redwood forest."

"Much obliged, pardner," the cowboy said. On his way out, he glanced back at Daniel. "You were saying?"

"He was just an old geezer," said Daniel. "What does he know?"

"More than you," the cowboy replied, turning a corner. Suddenly he stopped. A crowd of burly lumberjacks was blocking their path. They all had guns. One of the men stepped toward Daniel and held out his hand.

"We'll take that deed, kid," he said.

"How'd you know about that?" Pecos asked.

"Ain't you heard?" the lumberjack said. "There's a one-thousand-dollar reward offered for that piece of paper. Now, how about it, kid?"

SIX

The lumberjacks charged just as the cowboy grabbed at the railing of the catwalk and snapped a long chunk of it free. He swung it as hard as he could, knocking several of the loggers backward into the others. "Run!" the cowboy shouted to Daniel. At the other end of the catwalk, however, they blundered into another gang of lumberjacks.

Bang! Bang! The wood railing beside them splintered. They were being shot at.

"Hold on!" the cowboy shouted, grabbing a rope that dangled from the ceiling. Daniel threw his arms around the cowboy's waist, and the cowboy jumped off the catwalk and sailed down toward the floor below.

Halfway down, Daniel lost his grip.

"Help!" he shouted.

Wham! With a hard thud he fell onto one of the buzz saw's conveyor belts. He was headed straight for the gigantic blade. Daniel desperately tried to free himself, but his foot was caught under a log. In another few seconds he'd be sliced in two.

"*Mister!*" Daniel screamed. He looked everywhere for the cowboy. "Mister!

"PECOS!" Daniel cried finally.

As if by magic the cowboy appeared on a catwalk above Daniel. With a lightning-fast move he drew his pistols and fired.

Bang! Clang! . . . Bang! Clang! . . . Bang! Clang!

One after another the sharp teeth of the spinning blade were blasted away until the toothless saw smashed into a log and screeched to a halt.

Daniel managed to wrench his foot out from under the log just as Pecos joined him. They found themselves, however, backed into a corner of the lumber mill, surrounded by a hundred angry, greedy lumberjacks. There was no way out. All of a sudden a plank in the wall behind them opened, and the old geezer stuck his head out.

"This way!" he hissed. The lumberjacks opened fire.

Bang! Bang! Pecos and Daniel ran as hard as they could, dodging bullets left and right as they followed the old man down a short passageway. The next thing they knew, they were back outside being chased by another posse of men. As they ran, Pecos whistled for Widowmaker.

"*Ugh!*" The old geezer grunted suddenly and fell to the ground. Daniel gasped. A knife was buried in the old man's back. He looked up at Pecos and Daniel. "Tell Big

Paul that Sourdough Sam said so long. Tell him I was wrong—the old days *were* better."

The old man took one last breath, then collapsed. Daniel suddenly felt as if he were in some horrible dream. The old geezer was dead, just like his own pa might be dead. Just then, Widowmaker raced. Pecos jumped on the horse, pulled Daniel up behind him, and raced off in a hail of bullets.

It was dusk. Pecos and Daniel led Widowmaker on foot through a forest of redwoods so tall they seemed to disappear into the clouds.

"I've never seen a man die before," Daniel said somberly.

"How'd they know about us?" Pecos asked.

"Telegraph, I bet." Daniel caught Pecos's puzzled look and explained. "I read about it in a magazine. Strings of wire that let one person send codes to another person as far away as San Francisco or New York. And now there's a new invention called the telephone so they can actually hear each other's voices."

"Then everybody will know everybody else's business," Pecos said, sounding slightly horrified. "There won't be a place left where a man can have any privacy."

But Daniel had just realized something even more horrifying. "Now that this thousand-dollar reward for the deed to Pa's farm is on the telegraph, everybody and his brother's going to come after us."

"Used to be," Pecos said with a melancholy shake of his head, "a head start meant something."

"Least we got aw*aaaaaay!*" Without warning, Daniel was jerked by his feet and yanked straight up in the air. Pecos took a step to grab him, but the ground gave way and he tumbled into a deep pit.

"Whoa!" Daniel swayed upside down in the air, caught around the ankles by a rope snare. "Help!"

Thump! Thump! Thump! He heard a loud thrashing coming through the underbrush, something that sounded like footsteps, only much too loud.

"Ahhhhh!" Daniel screamed as a huge wet snout pressed against his face. The snout was connected to the biggest ox he'd ever seen—an ox as blue as a robin's egg!

"It ain't never enough for you termites, is it?"

The next thing Daniel knew, a huge, barrel-chested man with a great bushy beard and a ratty fur hat stomped toward him, carrying an enormous double-bitted ax. He was dressed in animal skins, and a long gray feather stuck out of his hat.

"It ain't enough you robbed me of my trade!" he boomed. "It ain't enough that I lost weight and can't sleep! Now you want my woods! You want it all! Well, I'm making my last stand! I'll go down swinging like a man!"

The giant lifted his huge ax as if to chop Daniel into little pieces.

"Pecos!" Daniel screamed.

The giant suddenly put down the ax. "Where?"

"Right here, you dumb ox!" Pecos shouted from the hole.

"Wooooo!" Insulted, the blue ox bellowed angrily.

"Not you, Babe!" Pecos quickly added. "I meant Paul."

"Why, Pecos Bill, you big bag of horse wind." The giant looked down into the pit and grinned. Then he reached down with one brawny arm and lifted Pecos out. "Let me take a gander at you. Still uglier than ever."

"At least I got some meat on my bones," Pecos said. "You're as thin as a rail, Paul. What happened?"

"Hard times, Pecos," the giant said, draping his arm over the cowboy's shoulders and starting to lead him away. "I'll tell you all about it over a jug."

"Excuse me," Daniel said, still swinging upside down. But the others ignored him.

"I was just thinking about you the other night," Paul said. "Remember that time in Silver City with them Sullivan sisters?"

"Hello?" Daniel called.

"Hard to forget," Pecos replied. "We lost a lot of sleep."

"Were there five or six of them?" Paul asked.

"Ahem." Pecos cleared his throat. "There's a young'un present."

The giant turned and regarded Daniel coldly. "So there is."

Daniel got the distinct impression that Paul Bunyan didn't care much for kids, but he decided to be friendly anyway. So he waved and said, "Pleased to meet you."

The giant answered with a mighty swing of his ax that sliced the rope that held Daniel's feet.

Thunk! Daniel fell headfirst to the ground. "Much obliged," grunted Daniel.

Paul led them to a cabin carved into the base of a huge redwood tree. While Pecos and Daniel ate a hearty meal, Paul contented himself with a jug of corn whiskey. Pecos told him about Sourdough Sam. Paul shook his head sadly.

"I warned him," he said. "They're not loggers. They're butchers with them fancy machines, cutting down everything in sight. They cut the sapling along with the full-growed so nothing will ever sprout again. Sourdough said I was behind the times. Me! Paul Bunyan, the man who invented logging."

Paul took a big gulp of whiskey and stood up. "Who thought up the double-bitted ax? Me, that's who! And who dreamed up the log flume? Me again! Maybe I'm old-fashioned, but in my day we didn't kill the land. We just borrowed from it."

"Well, what do you intend to do about it?" Pecos asked.

"I'll do what I darn well please," Paul snorted. "And the rest of the world can go to blazes."

"And Paradise Valley?" Pecos asked.

"No concern of mine." Paul shook his head.

Daniel glared at him. "You're not Paul Bunyan."

"Who says I ain't?" Paul snarled.

"My pa used to tell me stories about Paul Bunyan," Daniel said. "Paul was a giant of a man—a man who'd look danger in the eye and laugh in its face."

"He got that right," said Paul.

"Doesn't look that way to me," Daniel said. "Looks like you're just hiding out, feeling sorry for yourself."

Paul's eyes narrowed. He turned to Pecos. "Who is this sprout?"

"Sounds to me like you're just plain scared," Daniel said. "You're not the Paul Bunyan my pa told me about. You're just a big blowhard."

Bunyan glared at Daniel and made as if he was going to fight back. But then his shoulders sagged, and he slumped down wearily in a large chair. "You two got any idea what I been through?" he asked.

"What about what Sourdough Sam's been through?" Daniel asked.

"He's right, Paul," said Pecos.

Paul was quiet for a moment, brooding. He stared at Daniel. "How old are you, kid?" he asked.

"Twelve."

"Well, I'll come along," Paul said finally. "But I'm warning you," he told Daniel, "stay out of my way if you want to see thirteen."

•SEVEN•

The next morning at sunrise, Pecos and Daniel set out on Widowmaker, and Paul lumbered slowly behind on Babe.

"Hey, move it, you big blue bag of beef!" Pecos shouted irritably.

The huge blue ox bellowed angrily, and Paul patted him on the head. "It's okay, big fella. Papa's here. He won't let the bad man hurt you." To Pecos he added, "Watch your mouth! Babe's very sensitive."

They made their way out of the redwood forest and through the scrubland to the edge of civilization. Ahead of them stood a vast tent city on the shore of a flat gray river. The city was crisscrossed with muddy streets crowded with horses and wagons. At the center of the city were half a dozen wooden buildings and a tall wooden water tower. Fires burned in the open, and filthy children dressed in rags played in the streets.

"What is this place?" Paul asked, bewildered.

"Liberty City," Pecos replied. "A good example of the kind of mess these newfangled modern folk can make out of the land."

Just then a buggy roared past and honked.

Ahooga! Ahooga!

Widowmaker reared up apprehensively.

"It's okay," Daniel said. "It's just a horseless carriage."

Widowmaker settled down reluctantly. Even so, Daniel was pleased that Widowmaker had listened to him. He and Pecos dismounted and began walking, leading the horse by the reins. They passed a couple of saloons, a general store, a hotel, and a livery. But it was something outside the post office that made Daniel take notice: mixed in among the regular assortment of Wanted posters was a poster of *him*!

Glancing around nervously, Daniel hiked up his collar and followed close behind Pecos. Up ahead, a crowd of people had gathered around a man in a top hat.

"Who will try his hand against the latest miracle in modern technology?" the man bellowed. Pecos and Daniel pushed their way to the front of the crowd.

The man in the top hat was standing in front of a granite boulder with two metal spikes sticking out of it. Next to the boulder a man in overalls was busily oiling the gears of a fancy machine.

"I'm offering ten-to-one odds that this here machine can drive steel faster than any man alive!" crowed the man in the top hat. "Ain't anyone got the gumption to at least try?"

Just then a tall, muscular man stepped forward. He

was bare-chested and wore the overalls of a railroad man. Over his shoulder was slung an enormous sledge-hammer.

"My name's John Henry," the man said, holding out a fistful of dollars. "You've got yourself a bet."

Pandemonium broke out as one man after another clamored after the man in the top hat to lay down their bets. The odds jumped to twelve to one, then twenty to one that the steam drill would beat John Henry.

Then Pecos decided to up the ante.

"One hundred dollars, even money," he hollered above the crowd, "says John Henry here whips the contraption!"

Pecos was swamped by men wanting to take the bet. John Henry smiled. "Even money, Pecos? Can't you do better than that?"

"I don't know," Pecos replied with a grin. "That thingamabob looks like it means business."

"You ready?" the man in the top hat asked.

"I need a shaker," John Henry said. "Can't drive steel without one."

"Who'll turn the spike?" the man yelled.

The crowd fell silent.

"Whoever does'll be crushed like a bug by his hammer," the man next to Daniel whispered.

"Come on," urged the man in the top hat. "Someone's got to have the gumption."

"Oof!" Without warning, Widowmaker had butted Daniel with his snout, sending him sprawling forward.

"There's a brave lad," grinned the man in the top hat.

"Pecos!" whined Daniel.

But Pecos shook his head. "Sorry, Daniel, I got to protect my investment."

"But I can't," Daniel whimpered.

John Henry placed a reassuring hand on his shoulder. "You don't know till you've tried. You just grab hold of that spike and give it a quick shake and a turn each time I hit it."

"What if you miss?" Daniel asked.

"I never miss," John Henry replied. "Least, not yet."

The man in the top hat aimed his pistol in the air. "Ready! Set!" *Bang!* The race was on.

The steam drill sparked and sputtered to life. With engine chugging and wheels spinning, the steam drill began pounding the steel spike into the stone.

Meanwhile, John Henry seemed to be taking his time showing Daniel how to hold their spike.

"Just like that, son," he said when Daniel finally had it right. Then he swung his hammer high overhead in a sweeping arc.

Clang! The hammer came down on the spike so hard that the impact knocked Daniel on his rear end. John Henry helped him up.

"Now turn it, lad," he said, and swung again.

Clang! The spike sank another two inches into the rock. Daniel gave the spike a twist. John Henry swung his hammer again and again. The spike had almost disappeared into the stone when he pulled it out and called to Daniel.

"The two-foot jumper! And make it snappy!"

Meanwhile, the steam drill had already driven its spike two feet. John Henry was a foot behind!

Daniel grabbed a two-foot steel spike and jammed it in the hole.

"C'mon, John Henry!" someone yelled.

John Henry stopped his hammer in midswing and gazed into the crowd. "Why, Paul Bunyan," he said, "as I live and breathe."

"Live and breathe later!" Pecos shouted. "You got a race to win!"

John Henry turned to Daniel. "Guess it's time to get serious."

Clang! Clang! Clang! He started to swing harder and faster, and with each powerful stroke of John Henry's hammer the spike sank deeper and deeper into the rock. They finished the two-foot jumper and quickly replaced it with a three-footer. *Clang! Clang! Clang!* Then a four-footer. The man running the steam drill suddenly looked worried and turned a knob on the machine. The machine roared into overdrive.

Clang! Clang! Clang! John Henry's veins bulged, and sweat poured off his forehead. "The five-footer!" yelled John Henry.

Daniel was nearly exhausted. He struggled to lift the steel jumper, but it was just too heavy.

"I can't!" he gasped.

"You can!" John Henry shouted.

"They're too far ahead!" Daniel cried.

Cursing under his breath, John Henry pushed Daniel aside and took hold of the five-footer. He jammed it down into the boulder and resumed hammering. *Clang!*

Daniel looked over at the steam drill and shook his head. The spike had been hammered almost all the way through the rock.

"Go on, Daniel!" Pecos whispered fiercely.

Clang!

Daniel grabbed hold of the five-footer and gave it a turn.

John Henry had one final swing, and he put everything he had into it.

CLANG!

It was as if the granite boulder had exploded. John Henry's hammer came down so hard that the long spike shot clear through the boulder, shattering it into a million pieces. The crowd let out a thunderous cheer and surged toward them.

We won! Daniel thought. But the crowd ran past him to the man running the steam drill. As fast as John Henry had been, the machine had been faster. The machine had won!

John Henry used his forearm to wipe the sweat from his forehead and turned to Daniel. "We had them beat, boy," he said sadly.

Paul walked over and patted John Henry on the back. "You would've won for sure if it weren't for the kid. C'mon, you can buy me supper. I'm hungrier than a goat in a rock pasture."

Daniel watched the two men walk away. It's my fault we lost, Daniel thought miserably to himself. Pecos finished paying off his bets, then wandered over.

"I'm sorry," Daniel said.

"Did you give it your best shot?" Pecos asked. "If you did, you got nothing to be sorry for."

Daniel looked down at his feet. Had he given it his best shot? he wondered.

Pecos headed toward the saloon, but Daniel felt too low to do anything but stare at his own feet and feel sorry for himself. Then he felt something nudge his shoulder. It was Widowmaker.

"Go on," Daniel said bitterly. "You might as well get your licks in, too."

But Widowmaker shook his head and snorted softly, as if to say it was all right. Daniel managed a smile.

"Thanks, Widowmaker," he said. He felt a little better and decided to join Pecos at the saloon.

———————

The smoky saloon was crowded with men drinking and talking loudly. On the stage a mariachi band was playing off-key music. As Daniel walked up from behind, he overheard Paul whisper to Pecos that "the kid was bad news." Daniel coughed, and they stopped talking. Pecos handed Daniel a glass of sarsaparilla and raised his own for a toast.

"To the Code!" he said as all three men hoisted their glasses.

"To the Code!" Daniel raised his glass, but John Henry and Paul lowered theirs.

"What do you know about the Code?" John Henry asked.

"Plenty," Daniel said. "Pa's always going on about it."

"Knowing the Code ain't the same as living by it," Paul said. They raised their glasses again and chanted together: "Respect the land. Defend the defenseless. And don't never spit in front of women and children."

The three men spit at a spittoon, making it ring. Not to be left out, Daniel also spit. Only there was no ring. Instead, a huge mountain man angrily stepped toward him. Daniel looked down at the mountain man's boot and winced.

"You just stepped over the line, boy," the man growled, making a fist.

"Howdy, friend," Pecos said, quickly stepping between the mountain man and Daniel. "Can I buy you a drink?"

"Sure," the mountain man answered. "Soon as I'm done skinning this varmint."

"Holler if you need a hand," Paul said.

Pecos shot Paul a look as he tried to stay between the mountain man and Daniel. "You don't want to bother with this little saddle sore," Pecos told the mountain man. "He ain't worth your time."

"I'll be the judge of that," the man decided. He stepped toward Daniel, but Pecos stood his ground.

"I'd take that drink if I was you," John Henry warned the man.

Taking a look at John Henry, and realizing he was with Pecos, the mountain man seemed to reconsider. "Okay," he grumbled, "make it a whiskey."

Pecos raised his glass for another toast. "Gentlemen, to Texas, the nearest thing to heaven on God's green earth!"

The mountain man glared at Pecos and didn't lift his glass. "You from Texas?" he asked.

"I have that honor," Pecos replied.

The mountain man smirked. "Thought I smelled something funny in here."

Pecos bristled, and the mountain man shot him a nasty grin. Several of his burly companions had joined him. They appeared to be itching for a fight.

"Easy, Pecos," Paul said, resting his hand on his friend's shoulder. "I ain't had my supper yet."

Meanwhile, John Henry had rolled up his sleeves. He nodded at Daniel. "I'll say one thing for you, boy. You rub everybody the same way . . . the *wrong* way."

"Mister," Pecos asked the mountain man, "are you insulting the great state of Texas?"

"The great state of two-bit tinhorns, you mean," he replied. His friends snickered.

"Dang it, Pecos," Paul complained. "You know I can't scrap on an empty stomach."

Pecos ignored him and addressed the mountain man. "Mister, you can insult me. You can insult my friends. You can even insult my horse. But don't you ever insult the great state of Texas!"

The mountain man wound up and let go a haymaker right at Pecos's chin. *Slap!* Pecos caught his arm and stopped him cold. *Pow!* Pecos hit the mountain man in the jaw so hard he flew backward and smashed through the big glass window at the front of the saloon.

A brawl erupted, and Daniel watched awestruck as Pecos, Paul, and John Henry sent the rest of the mountain men sailing out of the saloon, one after another, followed by a couple of miners and cowboys for good measure. Tables were overturned, bottles were smashed, and men went flying every which way.

Bang! A shot went off near the doorway. Everybody froze. At the entrance of the saloon was a woman with a pistol in either hand. One of the pistols was smoking. Long blond hair fell out from under her brown hat, and on her vest was a silver sheriff's star.

"All right," she shouted, "everyone freeze!"

"Who's that?" Daniel whispered.

"Calamity Jane," John Henry whispered back.

● EIGHT ●

Anybody make a move and I'll fill him full of lead," Calamity Jane warned as she walked up to the bar. "Who started this confabulation?" she asked the bartender.

"Them two," he answered, pointing at Paul and John Henry. "There was a third one, too. Now, where'd he get to?"

Daniel was shocked to see Pecos crawling on his hands and knees toward the door.

In the mirror over the bar, Calamity Jane saw him sneaking away, too.

"Well, paint my toenails and curl my hair." She pulled her gun and aimed it behind her like a trick shooter.

Bang! She shot Pecos's hat right off his head. Shamefaced, Pecos stood up slowly with his hands raised.

"Hi, Calamity, my cactus flower," he said sweetly.

"Don't you cactus flower me, you double-crossing dog," Calamity muttered. She fired again.

Bang! Bang! The bullets whizzed past Pecos, who nervously backed toward the wall.

"I missed you, too, honey," Pecos said. "If you only knew."

"I know too well!" Calamity snapped. "You flea-infested little weasel!"

She fired again—*Bang! Bang! Bang!*—backing Pecos up a couple of steps.

"You're looking mighty pretty," Pecos said.

"Don't try and sweet-talk me, you gutless, brainless, heartless sidewinder!" Calamity fired again. Her bullets had drilled Pecos's outline into the wall behind him.

"Calamity, honey," Pecos whined, "you ain't still sore about Amarillo, are you?"

"You had to bring up Amarillo!" Her eyes narrowed, and she aimed her guns at Pecos.

Bang! Bang! Pecos's gun belt fell to the ground . . . along with his pants.

Daniel shook his head at the sight of the legendary Pecos Bill cowering against the wall in nothing but his long johns. Suddenly his losing earlier didn't seem quite so humiliating.

Later that night Daniel was sitting on the steps of the general store across from the Liberty City jail. Calamity Jane had locked up Pecos, Paul, and John Henry for starting the fight in the saloon. Daniel had learned from John Henry, however, that locking them up was mostly Calamity Jane's way of paying Pecos back for jilting her at the altar some years before.

Daniel watched a horse-drawn buggy pull up in front of the jail. A scrawny man carrying a bouquet of flowers jumped off and hurried inside. A few moments later he came out with Calamity, who was now wearing a dress, and her hair was all curled and pretty. The scrawny man helped her into the buggy, then they rode away.

Suddenly Daniel felt a hand clamp down hard on his shoulder. He twisted around and looked up into the face of an old drunk.

"Buy me a drink, huh, kid?" he asked.

"Some other time." Daniel jumped up and walked hurriedly away.

He turned a corner and bumped into a man wearing a plaid suit and carrying a gun.

"Watch where you're—," the man started to say. Then he stopped and squinted at Daniel. "Hey, ain't you that kid?"

Daniel turned and ran.

"Come back here!" the man shouted, running after him.

Cutting around corners and running down back alleys, Daniel managed to escape. Finally he stopped behind a darkened building to catch his breath.

Maaaawwwww! A loud bellow made him jump. What in the world? Daniel thought. He looked up at a sign that read Livery Stable.

Luckily for Daniel, nobody saw him lead Babe from the stable. It took some coaxing at first to get Babe to move at all until Daniel told him that Paul was in trouble.

Outside the jail, Daniel took the chain from Babe's harness and slipped it around the bars on the window.

"Okay, Babe," he whispered as he pulled on the ox's bridle. "Hoooo, ox! Hoooo, Babe!"

With a great heave the ox began pulling against the bars. Suddenly a face appeared at the window of the cell.

"So, Daniel Hackett," Pecos said with a big grin. "How's it feel to be on the other side of the law?"

"Fine," Daniel called back. "Just as long as my ma don't find out."

"Boy, I didn't think you had it in you," John Henry exclaimed, joining Pecos at the window.

"And that's *my* ox!" Paul added proudly.

Creaaakkkk! The entire cell slowly began to move off its foundation.

Roaaaaarrrrr! Daniel was suddenly distracted by an unfamiliar sound. They listened.

"Whatever it is," Pecos said, "it's coming this way."

Daniel had a bad feeling. He pulled on Babe's bridle. "Hoooo, ox! Hoooo, Babe!"

"Pull harder, you dumb ox!" Pecos yelled.

Babe stopped pulling, turned, and glared at Pecos.

Inside the cell, Paul groaned. "Why'd you have to go and say that?" he asked Pecos angrily. "Now you've hurt his feelings!"

Down the darkened street, however, Daniel could hear that the roaring sound was growing louder.

"Daniel!" John Henry shouted. "Behind you!"

Daniel turned. At least a dozen men in plaid suits

were roaring toward him in two- and four-wheel horse-less carriages. Daniel didn't know what to do.

"Run!" Pecos shouted. "Run, boy!"

Daniel ran, and just as the machines were about to cut him off, he ducked sideways off the street into a maze of tents. The machines overshot him and jammed on their brakes, fishtailing on the muddy street.

Daniel raced through the tent city as fast as he could, but the machines came right in after him. One of the men riding a two-wheeled machine roared up beside Daniel. He pulled his gun and aimed it. Just as he fired, the machine crashed into a tent.

Bang! The bullet whizzed past Daniel's head.

But the other machines were still close behind. Daniel tried to lose them by ducking down an alley. But the roar grew louder as they caught up to him. Daniel was ex-hausted. He couldn't keep running. This was it, he thought finally. It's over.

At the opposite end of the alley, however, Daniel saw a man chopping furiously at a telegraph pole with an ax. It was Paul!

The pole was starting to fall. Daniel ran as fast as he could.

"C'mon, Daniel!" Paul shouted. "Move it, boy!"

It's too far away, Daniel thought. He'd never make it before the pole fell. The men on their machines would catch him first. The pole was falling. Daniel put on one final burst of speed and dove. The pole crashed to the ground just as Daniel slipped under it.

"Hooo-hah! I'm Paul Bunyan!" Paul shouted merrily

as he watched one machine after another crash into the log. "I'm the greatest lumberjack of all time! I can outfight and outeat any man alive! I'm three hundred pounds of fury. I . . ."

Paul trailed off as a gang of toughs suddenly came crawling out from the wreckage. They ran after Daniel, pushing past Paul as if he didn't exist.

Daniel ran as fast as he could, but his legs were weak and his knees began to buckle from exhaustion. He turned down one last alley. It was a dead end. The alley ended with walls on three sides.

Daniel pressed himself helplessly against the far wall as the men appeared at the open end of the alley. His heart was beating like a steam drill, and he was gasping for breath. The men spread out in a semicircle and moved in for the kill. Daniel searched desperately for an escape, but there was nothing. One of the toughs stepped forward and reached for Daniel's neck.

Wham! The man was knocked off his feet by a telegraph pole!

In utter astonishment Daniel saw that Paul was swinging the pole as if it were a baseball bat.

Bam! Crunch! Two more men went down as Paul clobbered them. But by now a crowd of men surrounded him. The odds looked bad, Daniel thought, even for Paul Bunyan.

Suddenly Daniel felt a hand on his shoulder, and he was spun around. A man with a long scar on his face grinned at him. It was Stiles.

Daniel twisted out of his grip and ran. Stiles chased

after him. Daniel was exhausted, and Stiles was catching up fast. Finally Daniel staggered to a stop down a side street. He had to catch his breath. With a nasty smile, Stiles stepped toward him. Once again Daniel was cornered. He faked as if to run, but Stiles wasn't fooled. He stepped closer. Daniel looked around. To his left was a wooden ladder that led up to a water tower. But there was no place to run. Stiles took another step, and Daniel knew what he had to do. The only way out . . . was up.

● NINE ●

Daniel scrambled up the ladder to the water tower with Stiles right behind him. He reached the walkway that ran around the huge barrel on top of the tower. Stiles followed him, and they stood facing each other.

"Nobody's going to hurt you, son," Stiles promised Daniel. "Just hand over the deed."

"You shot Pa!" Daniel shouted. He gasped and backed away nervously.

"That was his doing, not mine," Stiles replied coolly. "I tried to settle things in a peaceable way. All he had to do was sell the deed."

"He didn't have to do anything!" Daniel shouted. "It's his land!"

"Your pa was a fool," Stiles growled between clenched teeth. "He's stuck in the past and wants you to be stuck with him. You want to waste your life stuck behind a plow?"

Daniel shook his head.

"I bet you hate that farm," Stiles said, stepping closer. "It's a dried-up, miserable piece of land."

Daniel hesitated.

"Give me the deed!" Stiles's hand shot out like a snake, but Daniel quickly jerked back.

"You're trying my patience, son." Stiles's eyes narrowed, and he reached to his belt and pulled out a knife. Daniel backed against the wooden railing and looked down. There was no escape. Stiles stepped closer, and the blade of his knife glinted in the moonlight.

"Now," Stiles ordered, "hand it over like a good little boy."

Whack! Out of nowhere a hatchet slammed into the side of the water tower, pinning the sleeve of Stiles's coat to the wood. Daniel looked down and saw Paul a few rungs below, waving.

"Jump, Daniel!" he shouted.

Daniel hesitated. Meanwhile, Stiles had wrenched the hatchet free. Water gushed from the hole as Stiles reached back to hurl the hatchet. At the last second Daniel jumped off the water tower.

Ahhhhhh! Ripppp! Crash! Paul caught Daniel and they fell, landing on a tent in a tangle of canvas and ropes.

"Kid," Paul muttered. "Trouble seems to follow you like a bird dog."

"Lucky for me I got friends," Daniel replied.

"We ain't that good friends," Paul said, pushing Daniel off him. "Get your mangy carcass off me!"

Chopping wood is one of twelve-year-old Daniel Hackett's boring farm chores.

Daniel is surprised when he finds himself way downriver from Paradise Valley.

Daniel is rescued by legendary tall tale figure Pecos Bill!

That night around a campfire, Daniel tells Pecos about his family's problems.

Trapped on a lumber mill's conveyor belt, Daniel is heading straight for a buzz saw!

Daniel holds the spike steady as John Henry prepares to swing his hammer.

Calamity Jane uses her six-guns to make a point about law and order.

John Henry, Pecos Bill, and Paul Bunyan grin through the bars of the jail.

It looks like there's no escape when the corrupt Stiles traps Daniel on a water tower.

Pecos leads Daniel, Paul, and John Henry across the desert on their way back to Paradise Valley.

An injured Jonas Hackett surprises Daniel by agreeing to sell the farm to Stiles.

Daniel attempts to single-handedly hold back the oncoming train!

With one mighty swing of an ax, Daniel brings the train tunnel crashing down.

It's time to say good-bye, and Paul Bunyan gives Daniel a bear-size hug.

Daniel is proud to take the reins of Widowmaker, Pecos Bill's legendary horse.

Bang! A wooden tent pole next to them shattered into splinters. Daniel looked up. Half a dozen men with guns were running toward him.

"Kill them!" Stiles screamed as he climbed down from the water tower. "Kill them both!"

Paul and Daniel ran off down the street.

"How'd you get out of jail, anyway?" Daniel asked as they ran.

"Pecos apologized to Babe, and he pulled the wall down," Paul said. "Now we got to get ourselves to the ferry."

They raced to the docks. But this time it was Paul who fell behind. At the dock Daniel could see Pecos and John Henry leading Babe and Widowmaker onto a large log raft.

As John Henry cast off, Daniel leaped onto the raft just as it started to drift away from the dock.

"C'mon, Paul!" Daniel shouted. Paul was huffing and puffing as he ran along the dock. "You can do it!" Daniel yelled.

Paul reached the edge of the dock and jumped. He flew through the air and went sprawling onto the raft.

Meanwhile, Stiles's men had reached the dock and had begun shooting. Pecos was shooting back.

Suddenly Daniel saw a man climb out from behind a barrel on the raft. It was one of Stiles's men, and his gun was aimed at Pecos.

Bang! A distant shot rang out. And before Daniel could even warn Pecos, the other man slumped and tumbled into the water.

Everyone stared up at a far-off cliff where a woman with a rifle stood silhouetted in the moonlight.

"Calamity!" Pecos shouted, and waved. Calamity Jane waved back, then walked away.

———————

For the rest of the night, weary from all the excitement, Daniel slept as the raft drifted slowly downriver.

The next day Daniel fished off the back of the raft with a pole made from a long, thin tree branch. That afternoon John Henry sat down beside him and let his feet trail in the water.

"Thinking about your pa?" he asked.

Daniel looked up, surprised. How did John Henry know? he wondered.

"I used to bait a line with my daddy when I was young," John Henry said. "I never caught much, but that wasn't the point."

"Seems like fishing is the only time me and Pa get along," Daniel said. "Otherwise, I can't do nothing right."

"My daddy was the same way," John Henry said. "He was always telling me what to do like I didn't have a mind of my own."

"Exactly!" Daniel agreed.

"Now I see that he only bothered because he cared so much," John Henry said. "He was just doing the best he knew how."

Daniel realized that he had never thought about it that way. Maybe John Henry was right, Daniel thought.

"The thing I feel the worst about is never having the chance to tell him," John Henry said. "We was slaves, and he got sold down the river. It's too late for me," he said, looking Daniel straight in the eye. "But maybe not for you."

Toward evening they beached the raft on the riverbank and climbed uphill to make camp. Up ahead was one of the most fantastic sights Daniel had ever beheld. He and the others stood in the red light of the setting sun and gazed into the mouth of an enormous cavern that was crisscrossed with golden shafts of light that seemed to disappear far into the darkness.

"I've seen many a wondrous sight," John Henry said reverently. "But none held a candle to this."

"We'll make camp here," Pecos said as he uncinched Widowmaker's saddle.

Daniel and the men shared dinner. Later, while Paul chopped wood for the fire and John Henry played softly on a harmonica, Pecos brushed Widowmaker down and told Daniel the story of how he had found him. He had heard stories about the horse for years, Pecos said, long before finally tracking him down.

"He bucked and twisted and spun for about three months," Pecos recollected fondly. "He couldn't unseat me, and I couldn't tame him. Finally I was getting kind of thirsty and asked if he'd stop for a drink. Widowmaker agreed, and we pretty much been partners ever since."

"If you two are done jawing," Paul interrupted, tossing some split wood to Daniel, "there's some wood for the fire."

Daniel knew he had something to say to Paul, and after he picked up the wood he walked up to him. "I just wanted to say thanks for saving my life yesterday," he told Paul.

Paul shrugged. "I'd do the same thing for a stray cat."

"I guess I've been nothing but trouble for everybody," Daniel said.

Paul studied him for a moment. "You ain't been *that* bad," he said. "For a kid."

That made Daniel smile. True, it wasn't much, Daniel thought, but it meant a lot coming from Paul. Daniel picked up some wood and carried it back to the fire.

It was a clear, moonlit night.

"I once seen a picture of New York City at night," Daniel said, throwing a log on the fire. "It was all lit up with electric lightbulbs. Wish we had a few of them right now."

"Electric lightbulbs?" Pecos said, and scowled.

"Little balls of glass with light a hundred times brighter than a candle," Daniel said.

"Go on!" John Henry said.

"It's true," Daniel said. "Pretty soon people will just flip a switch to light up a house. There won't be no darkness no more. It'll be like noon at midnight."

"Then how'll folks see the stars?" John Henry asked.

"They just won't," Daniel said.

"Well, I don't like it," Pecos said firmly. "And what's more, I think it's nothing but a tall tale."

"You're right," John Henry said with a laugh. "Daniel here's just pulling our legs."

"It's the God's honest truth!" Daniel insisted.

The men stopped laughing and glanced at one another.

"Not see the stars?" Pecos asked, looking up at the stars twinkling in the sky. Daniel looked up, too. For the first time he realized what a shame that would be.

After a while Daniel got up.

"Where're you going?" Pecos asked, looking up from the fire.

"Just want to take a closer look around," Daniel said. All evening Daniel had been curious about what he might find in the cavern.

Just inside the cavern, the light from the fire shimmered against the rock wall. It looked to Daniel as if the rock were made of gold. He'd never seen anything like it. Deeper inside the cavern the firelight began to dim, but his curiosity grew stronger.

Suddenly Daniel thought he heard something. He squinted into the dark. Nothing there, Daniel decided. He went a few more feet.

Rrrrrrrrrrrr . . .

A low, soft grumble seemed to come up from out of nowhere. Maybe it was just Paul's stomach grumbling, Daniel thought. He went a few feet more, then heard a soft scratching sound.

Daniel stopped. He couldn't see a thing, but he had the feeling he was not alone in the cavern. He started to slowly back up. Suddenly he felt a warm breath on the back of his neck. Daniel whirled around just as a huge beast shot out of the shadows and reared up on its hind legs. Daniel froze in terror. The beast had the fierce eyes of a grizzly, the massive horns of an elk, and the gleaming fangs of a mountain lion.

"Ahhhhhhhhh!" Daniel screamed. He clamped his eyes shut, expecting the end.

But nothing happened.

Daniel opened one eye, then the other. He sighed with relief. The cavern was empty. Just in case, however, he turned and ran out as fast as he could.

"What's wrong?" Pecos asked when Daniel ran up to the fire. He was gasping for breath. "You look like you've seen a ghost."

Daniel glanced back at the cavern. He knew what he'd seen, Daniel thought. Or what he'd *thought* he'd seen.

"I didn't see nothing," he decided finally. "Nothing, you hear? I couldn't have!"

Pecos, Paul, and John Henry exchanged amused expressions as Daniel crawled into his bedroll. He muttered a quick good-night, but it was quite a while before he fell asleep.

TEN

The following morning they broke camp and headed out down a mountainside and across an arid, empty plain. The sun was burning hot. Along the way they passed the scarred wreckage of a rusted, windblown wagon. In the sand beside the wagon lay the skeletons of a man, woman, and child.

Looking at the skeleton of the child, Daniel wondered if he would wind up the same way.

As they rode on, the sun got hotter and hotter. Paul opened a canteen for a refreshing sip of water, but only sand spilled out. "Great," he said. "We're out of water."

"This is nothing compared to the summer of 1888," Pecos said. "It got so hot, the chickens were laying fried eggs. Things got so bad the entire state of Texas caught on fire. I had to lasso a twister to get a ride out of there."

Paul gave him a sour look. "Here I am lost in the middle

of a giant barbecue pit," he grumbled. "I don't know what'll kill me first. The heat or listening to Pecos's stories."

"Simmer down, you two," John Henry said. "Fighting won't help anything."

"Stay out of this, you loser," Paul muttered.

"One time I lost!" John Henry said defensively. "One measly time."

"Cost me a bundle," Pecos said.

"I suppose you could do better?" John Henry yelled.

"That's telling him!" shouted Paul.

"Shut up, you big tub of lard!"

John Henry pushed Paul. The three men started to push and shove one another, but Daniel hardly noticed. His attention was riveted ahead where rippling waves of heat rose from the ground. A figure was making its way toward them through the scrub and sand.

There was something very familiar about it.

"Pa!" Daniel shouted. He started to run. "Pa! It's me, Daniel!"

He kept running and shouting. "Daniel!" his father called back, holding out his arms. He, too, started to run.

Daniel couldn't believe it. He had found his father right here in the desert!

But just as Daniel was about to embrace his father, he disappeared. Daniel stumbled and fell into the dirt.

"Pa!" he cried, clawing at the sand with his hands. "Pa?"

"It was a mirage," Pecos said, running up from behind.

"No! He was there!" Daniel cried. "He yelled to me."

"It's amazing the things the heat can do to a man," Pecos said.

For Daniel, however, it was the last straw. He'd lost all hope. "I ain't never gonna make it back to Paradise Valley!"

"Sure you will," said Pecos.

"I say we turn back," Daniel cried. "I'll give Stiles the stupid deed."

"What about the farm?" John Henry asked. "What about your promise to your pa?"

"We wouldn't be in this mess if it weren't for him," Daniel said angrily. "He cares more about the farm than he does Ma, Eli, or me. He just cares about himself!"

Pecos kicked the dirt, and spit. "Well," he said. "Things can't get no worse than this."

One by one the men walked on ahead. Daniel felt tears roll down his cheeks. Finally he wiped his eyes on his shirtsleeve, climbed to his feet, and trudged off after them.

But things did get worse. Toward midday they were hit by a sandstorm. Protecting their faces with bandannas, they struggled against the swirling sand that stung like needles. Later they camped on the edge of a steep cliff. Pecos was so tired he asked Daniel if he'd water and brush Widowmaker. Daniel was exhausted, too. But he agreed. When Widowmaker allowed Daniel to take his reins, Daniel couldn't help but feel just a little bit proud.

He was hiding in a long, dark railroad car decorated with plush red fabrics and ornate lanterns. Portly men smoking cigars and wearing suits with gold watch chains were shouting at Stiles to get the deed. Suddenly Stiles turned and pointed his pearl-handled pistols at Daniel. . . .

"Don't shoot!" Daniel screamed. "Don't shoot me!"

Daniel jackknifed up in his bedroll. It was a dream. He looked across the fading embers of the fire at Paul and John Henry, who were sound asleep. Farther away, sitting guard near the edge of the cliff, was Pecos.

Daniel got up and walked over to him. Pecos spun around and drew his gun. When he saw that it was Daniel, he lowered it.

"Couldn't sleep?" Pecos asked.

Daniel shook his head. "I've been thinking about tomorrow. Do you think they'll be waiting for us?"

"More than likely," Pecos said. "You scared?"

Daniel nodded.

"Me, too," said Pecos.

Daniel was surprised. "I didn't think you were afraid of anything."

"It's overcoming fear that's the real mark of a man," Pecos said. "Not denying it exists. It's believing so strong in something, you're willing to put your life on the line."

"What are you afraid of, Pecos?" Daniel asked.

"Well, I guess what scares me most is that maybe I don't got what it takes anymore. Maybe the old days—my days—are fading a little too fast." He looked over at Daniel. "What are you afraid of, son?"

"Well," Daniel said, "besides getting blown to kingdom come tomorrow, I guess I'm afraid of not doing the right thing."

"You'll do the right thing," Pecos assured him.

"How will I know?" Daniel asked.

"You'll know."

They sat quietly for a little while, enjoying the peaceful silence.

Somewhere, an animal cried.

Ahhhhhhhwwwwoooooooo!

"What's that?" Daniel asked. He knew he'd heard it once before, but he couldn't remember where.

Pecos pointed to a cliff on the other side of the river. There, profiled against the moon, was an animal that looked to be part buffalo, part grizzly, and part mountain lion, but with the horns of an elk.

Daniel's eyes widened. "A cliffside grounder!" he gasped. "What's he saying?"

"He's calling to see if there's any of his kind left out there," Pecos said. He shook his head sadly. "But there ain't. He's the last of his breed. Pretty soon he'll be gone, too. But that don't mean he never was."

Pecos turned and studied Daniel for a moment in the dark. "Better scoot. We've got a big day tomorrow, and you'll need some shut-eye."

Daniel walked back to his bedroll and climbed inside. He looked back at Pecos. Sitting there with his Winchester cradled in his arms, Daniel thought Pecos looked small in the pale glow of moonlight.

Like the cliffside grounder, Daniel wondered if Pecos Bill was the last of his breed.

• ELEVEN •

Something hard and cold was pressed against his forehead. Daniel awoke with a start and found himself staring down the barrel of a pistol. Dawn was already turning the sky gray. Stiles leaned over him with a mean smile.

"Morning, boy," he said.

Daniel nervously glanced sideways. Pecos, Paul, and John Henry were surrounded by a dozen men with rifles and had been forced to stand back-to-back with their hands up.

"They got the drop on me, Daniel," Pecos said. "Snuck up when I weren't looking, too," he snarled. "Them dirty varmints!"

Stiles grabbed Daniel's collar and yanked him to his feet, keeping his pistol pressed against the boy's head. "The deed, son."

"Harm one hair of that boy and you're a dead man," Pecos warned.

"I got no quarrel with you or your friends," Stiles said. "I just want that deed."

Daniel was in no position to argue. Despite the shocked and surprised look Pecos gave him, he started to reach into his pocket, saying, "We don't have a prayer, Pecos. We never did."

"If that's your way of thinking, I reckon you're right," Pecos replied grimly.

Daniel looked away.

"You can't stop progress," Stiles said, addressing Pecos. "The difference between you and me is I can adjust to the times and you can't."

"Don't listen to him, Daniel," Paul said.

"We can win this thing yet," said John Henry.

"You just got to believe," Pecos urged him.

But Daniel would have none of it. "Where do you come off telling me what to do or how to live?" he demanded of them angrily.

"That's it, boy!" Stiles cheered. "That's the spirit!"

"Don't do it, Daniel," Pecos said.

"You're just a bunch of crazy tall tales my pa made up," Daniel yelled back. John Henry and Paul looked shaken. Even Pecos looked stunned.

"I'm a ring-tailed roarer!" Pecos insisted, trying to make Daniel listen. "I can draw faster, shoot straighter, and ride harder than any man alive."

Daniel sadly shook his head. "You're nothing but hot air."

"I don't have all day, boy!" Stiles growled, holding out his hand for the deed. "Time is money."

Daniel reached deeper into his pocket. "I just want to go home," he tried to explain to Pecos.

"I'm the ripsnortingest cowboy who ever rode north, south, east, or west of the Rio Grande," Pecos said. But his eyes had grown dull and lifeless, and he had to struggle to say the words. To Daniel it seemed almost as if the life was being drained out of Pecos.

But what could he do? Daniel pulled out the deed and handed it to Stiles.

"I knew you'd see it my way," he said smugly.

Suddenly the wind kicked up, swirling wildly, whipping up dust and dirt. Daniel covered his eyes. For a moment he couldn't see a thing. Then, just as fast as it had started up, it calmed down. Daniel took his hands away from his eyes and looked around.

There was no one there.

Daniel looked around in astonishment. Stiles and his men were gone. Pecos, John Henry, and Paul had vanished, too. Daniel was alone on the edge of the cliff. It felt as if he were standing on the edge of the world.

"Pecos?" he cried. *"Pecooooooosssss!"*

No one answered. Daniel noticed a trail leading down the face of the cliff. That's where Pecos and the others must have gone! He started down the trail, stumbling and sliding in the loose gravel and rock. Up ahead he could hear the faint roar of machinery.

The sound grew louder as Daniel continued down the trail. It was coming from right around an outcropping of rock. Daniel started to run.

He came around the bend and suddenly skidded to a

stop. Before him stretched an unbelievable sight: a broad, blackened valley crisscrossed with train tracks and covered with churning oil wells. A dirty cloud of smoky haze hung in the air, and the ground was littered with abandoned machines and pockmarked with huge piles of oil-blackened earth.

Daniel was shocked. Past a sluggish river clogged with brackish water and garbage, Daniel found dozens of grim-faced workers hacking at the earth, laying down more track. To the side, Daniel noticed a wooden sign that had fallen over. He kneeled down. In faded letters Daniel read the words Welcome to Paradise Valley.

No! Daniel thought. *It can't be!*

Why had he given Stiles the deed? he wondered. Now he could see that it was the worst thing he'd ever done.

Clang! A bell rang, and immediately the workers dropped their tools and began to trudge single file past Daniel. A vaguely familiar figure was coming toward him. He was wearing tattered, filthy clothes. The man's shoulders slumped, and his eyes stared out vacantly at the world without seeing.

No! Daniel thought. *Not Pa! Nooooooo!*

———————

KA-BOOM! A huge explosion shook the earth.

"Noooooo!" Daniel shouted, and opened his eyes. He was lying in a rowboat. For a moment he didn't know where he was. Looking around, he realized the boat was tied to the dock. The river around him was still blue. He was back in Paradise Valley! *But what about*

Stiles? He reached into his pocket. The deed was still there.

"Pa!" Daniel gasped, suddenly remembering his father. He quickly climbed out of the boat and started to run back toward the house. Ahead he could see his mother standing on the porch.

"Ma!" Daniel shouted, and waved. "I made it back!"

As if his wish had come true, his mother turned and smiled. "Your father's going to be all right, Daniel."

Daniel raced past her into the house. His father was lying in bed, pale and drawn, but when he saw his son, a slight grin creased his lips.

Daniel was so happy that he threw his arms around his father's neck.

"Pa, I'm sorry!" he gasped.

"It's all right, Daniel." Jonas patted his shoulder softly. "I knew you didn't mean what you said."

"I told Pecos you were a fool," Daniel confessed. "I told him you were stupid for standing up against Stiles. But I was the fool."

"Pecos?" his father asked.

"Pecos Bill," Daniel said as if it were obvious.

"You talked to Pecos Bill?" Jonas asked.

"And Paul Bunyan and John Henry," Daniel said. "They was just like you said they'd be, Pa."

"Where was this?" his father asked.

Daniel told him the story of Pecos and his friends, of going to the redwood forest, Liberty City, and the great cavern, and how Stiles and his men had finally caught them.

"And the deed?" Jonas asked.

"It's right here," Daniel said, patting his pocket. "And the valley's still here, and we have to save it!"

His mother and father gave each other troubled glances.

"You don't believe me?" Daniel said.

"You fell asleep in the boat," his mother reminded him.

"But they were there!" Daniel insisted, turning to his father. "They was as real as you and me! Pa, you believe me, don't you?"

Jonas patted his son's hand. "I believe you."

KA-BOOM! There was another explosion in the distance.

"Not that it matters anymore," his father added. "We're selling. Your ma's right. No piece of ground is worth dying for."

"You mean you're giving up?" Daniel asked.

"*Wising* up," his father corrected him.

"But you'll be leaving the land defenseless!" Daniel cried. "We can't give in, Pa. You know what they'll do!"

Daniel felt his mother's hands on his shoulders. "Now, Daniel," she said gently but firmly, "you heard your father. Let him rest."

"But somebody's got to stop them!" Daniel protested.

"Come away now," she said as she led Daniel out of the room.

———————

KA-BOOM!!

Daniel was sitting on the edge of the porch, listening to the explosions, trying to figure out what to do. If only

Pecos were there to help him. Just then a gust of wind blew past, and Daniel's head jerked up. "Pecos?"

A horse nearby neighed.

"Widowmaker?" Daniel looked around excitedly, but it was only Samson whinnying at the strange breeze.

Daniel stared down at his feet. He had to face facts. Pecos wasn't going to come and help him, he realized. This was one problem he'd have to face alone.

But was it *really* worth it? Daniel wondered. After all, even his father was ready to give up. Daniel gazed out from the porch to the fields of tall golden grass that swayed lazily in the breeze. Farther off, the clear blue river flowed past its tree-lined banks.

And then, just like that, Daniel knew just what he had to do.

•TWELVE•

KA-*BOOM!* The thud of explosions grew more intense as Daniel got closer to town. It seemed as if everyone in Paradise Valley were standing on the wood-plank sidewalks, staring up at the huge hole the railroad workers had blasted in the side of the mountain.

Some townsfolk pointed and muttered as Daniel walked past them down the center of the street. Daniel climbed up the gravel incline to the train tracks and started to walk along them. The railroad workers stopped hammering spikes and stared at him, too.

Ahead loomed the dark, gaping mouth of the tunnel. As Daniel marched toward it, he could hear the rumble of an approaching train. Now he could see it heading toward him, a huge black mechanical monster belching gray smoke and white steam.

Daniel's heart was thumping in his chest, but it was

too late to turn back. He stopped in the middle of the tracks and held out his hand.

Screeech! The train's brakes locked, and the huge iron wheels shrieked and spit sparks. Daniel squeezed his eyes shut. He didn't know if the train would stop in time or not.

The train stopped, and Daniel opened his eyes. The engine's huge iron grille was just inches in front of him.

The locomotive's engineer stuck his head out a side window and stared at Daniel. Out of the corner of his eye Daniel noticed that the townsfolk had climbed up the incline and stood watching.

Now Stiles came running forward from one of the cars behind the locomotive. His face was streaked with shaving cream, and he was pulling on his gun belt. It was obvious that he'd been in the middle of a shave. When he saw Daniel blocking the tracks, he was incredulous. Then he smiled.

"I see your pa's sent a boy to do a man's job."

"I came on my own accord," Daniel replied. "You and your kind ain't welcome in Paradise Valley."

Stiles glared at him. "Get off the tracks, boy."

"No." Daniel stood firm.

"I'm warning you," Stiles said. "Get off."

"And I'm warning *you,*" Daniel replied, bracing himself. "Get out of Paradise Valley."

"You think you can stop us?" Stiles asked.

"Maybe not, but I'll give it my best shot."

"Have it your way," Stiles said, climbing up onto the

front of the locomotive and waving up at the engineer. "Run him over!"

The engineer just stared back at him.

"I said run him over!" Stiles shouted.

"I can't run over a kid," the engineer shouted back.

"You can!" Stiles screamed. "And you will!"

The engineer's face disappeared inside the cab of the locomotive. The engine began to roar, and with a great hiss of steam the brakes were released. The train slowly inched forward. Daniel pressed his hands against the bars of the cold iron grille and began to push back.

Daniel began to backpedal. He was no match for the huge machine. The train started to move faster. Daniel was just holding on now, trying to keep from falling. Suddenly he staggered and fell backward. A loud gasp rose up from the crowd of railroad workers and towns-folk. In another second the train's huge wheels would crush him. This was it. Daniel shut his eyes.

Creak! The train suddenly stopped. Daniel looked up. John Henry was standing over him, his muscled arms trembling as he single-handedly held back the train. Daniel quickly scrambled to his feet.

"What the heck?" Stiles shouted, looking down from the front of the engine. Meanwhile, Daniel joined John Henry and started to push.

"Where have you been?" Daniel asked John Henry matter-of-factly.

"Just waiting for you to make your move," John Henry replied with a wink.

"Kill them!" Stiles shouted, waving down the tracks to

where forty armed men were running toward Daniel and John Henry with guns flopping at their sides.

"Hold it right there," a voice called out to the men. Daniel turned around and smiled. Pecos, his eyes fixed ahead, stood facing down the tracks with both hands twitching over his six-guns. Stiles's men skidded to a stop. The lead man stepped forward warily. Daniel recognized him. It was the man in the black derby, the one he'd seen outside Sheriff Peters's office.

"I don't know who you are," he told Pecos. "But we got no fight with you."

"No, defenseless kids and farmers are more your style," Pecos spit back.

The man's eyes narrowed. "Mister, you just got yourself killed!"

He nodded at the men, who spread out, lowering their hands over their guns. It was one man against forty. Daniel bit his lip. The odds were hopeless.

Everyone went for their guns at once.

Pow! Pow! Pow! Pow! Pecos's guns blazed.

"Ahhhhhhhhhhh!" screamed forty men as they all clutched their wounded hands.

Pecos grinned as all forty turned and ran. He calmly blew the smoke away from his pistols.

Meanwhile, Stiles had turned beet red. "More steam!" he shouted at the engineer. *"More steam!"*

The train began to chug as it picked up speed.

"Come on!" one of the townsmen shouted when he saw John Henry straining. "What are we waiting for!"

A swarm of townsfolk hurried up the incline to join

Pecos, John Henry, and Daniel as they tried to push back the locomotive.

"More steam!" Stiles screamed.

"She's giving all she's got!" the engineer cried as the crowd slowly began to push the locomotive back into the tunnel.

Stiles reached into his pocket and pulled out a fistful of cash.

"I'll give you one hundred dollars an acre!" he shouted. "Even a hundred fifty an acre!"

But the townsfolk ignored him and kept pushing. A bunch of portly, expensively dressed men jumped from one of the train's cars and began to run.

"Where's Paul?" Daniel asked Pecos as they pushed the train back into the tunnel.

"Oh, he's around," Pecos replied with a smile and a wink. The train's brakes began to give, and the engineer jumped from the locomotive. The crowd gave the train one final push, and it began to roll backward into the dark.

"And stay out!" Daniel shouted.

Suddenly, inside the tunnel, there was a great rumbling. Rocks and dirt began to fall just as Paul Bunyan lumbered out of the darkness carrying his ax.

"Stand back!" he shouted to the crowd as he stopped next to the last wooden tunnel support. "One more ought to do it!"

Daniel realized that Paul had been chopping down the supports inside the tunnel.

"Let me!" he yelled to Paul.

The big man looked surprised but handed Daniel his huge ax. The ax was so heavy Daniel had to drag it over the ground to the final tunnel support, which was groaning and shuddering under the weight of the mountain. Daniel stopped and rubbed some dirt in his hands.

"Wait!" a voice cried. Daniel turned and saw Stiles stagger out of the darkness. "Be reasonable, boy," the man gasped. "You know we'll win in the end."

Daniel stared back at him coldly. "Maybe, maybe not," he replied, and started to pick up the ax.

"Name your price," he said. "I'll pay whatever you want!"

"I ain't interested," Daniel said, straining to raise the ax over his head.

"You fool!" Stiles cried. "There'll be others after me. As long as there's a profit to be made, we'll keep coming."

"Not through *our* land!" Daniel shouted as he brought down the ax.

Crack! The blade smashed through the last beam.

"Timmmmmmmberrrrrr!" Daniel yelled gleefully. The tunnel began to collapse. Daniel started to run, then looked behind him. Stiles was standing as stiff as a statue, with his gun drawn and aimed right at him.

Crunk! Just as Stiles was about to pull the trigger, a huge rock hit him on the shoulder, knocking him to his knees.

ROOAAARRRRR! A second later the entire tunnel collapsed, and Stiles disappeared beneath a hail of rock and dirt and dust.

"We did it!" Daniel shouted. "We did it!"

"We sure did." Daniel felt a hand on his shoulder and looked up, expecting to find Paul Bunyan. But it was just Mr. Bronson, his father's friend.

Daniel quickly looked around for Pecos, Paul, and John Henry. But they had vanished once again.

• THIRTEEN •

The next day Daniel and his father walked along the neat, straight furrows of the north field, throwing down seed for the next season's crop. His father had one arm in a sling. It was dusk, and the sky was filled with soft pink clouds. The snow-covered peaks surrounding Paradise Valley shimmered in the golden sunset. It was hard to imagine a place that looked more beautiful.

"Right nice sunset, huh, Pa?" Daniel asked.

"Sure is," Jonas said. "Well, time to call it a day and get some supper."

"You go ahead," Daniel replied, breathing in the cool evening air. "I think I'll just stay here for a while."

His father seemed to understand and walked alone back to the farmhouse.

"Pa?" Daniel called out to his father. He stopped and turned. Daniel smiled. "I love you, Pa."

Jonas smiled. "I love you, too, Son."

Daniel was not at all surprised to find Pecos Bill, Widowmaker, Paul Bunyan, Babe, and John Henry all standing near the edge of the field.

"We come to say good-bye," Pecos said, taking off his hat.

"I knew you would," Daniel said. He moved closer and held out his hand to Paul. "Thanks."

"And thank *you*, Daniel," he said.

"Me?" Daniel couldn't imagine why Paul would thank him.

"Thanks to you I got my old appetite back," Paul said. "I figure I'll head up to Alaska. I hear they got country up there that still ain't half-growed yet."

Then Paul pulled Daniel into a crushing hug. Next Daniel turned to John Henry.

"I've been thinking about a rematch with that steam drill," he told Daniel.

"Think you'll need a shaker?" Daniel asked.

"If I do, I know where to find one." John Henry smiled and gave Daniel a hug, too.

"To the Code!" Daniel said.

"To the Code!" the three men cheered.

Pecos Bill and Daniel watched John Henry and Paul walk away across the field until they both shimmered, grew dim, and disappeared.

Daniel looked up into Pecos Bill's face.

"I'm much obliged, Daniel," Pecos said.

"You're the one who did everything," Daniel replied.

"You done right, son," Pecos said. "I was near convinced

that weren't possible no more. Now I know I can rest easy."

Widowmaker neighed and rubbed his muzzle against Daniel, who patted him gently.

"So long, Widowmaker," he whispered.

"Hop on," Pecos said.

"What?" Daniel asked, surprised.

"Figured you might want to take a ride before I hit the trail," Pecos said.

Daniel turned to Widowmaker. "Is that okay with you?"

Widowmaker snorted and nodded. Pecos boosted Daniel up and slapped the horse on the rump.

"Git, boy!" They took off together at a full gallop. Daniel did all he could to stay in the saddle, feeling Widowmaker charging beneath him and the wind in his face.

Around them the wind whipped up mightily, shaking the trees and making the long grass ripple like waves on the ocean.

Daniel saw that a twister had suddenly kicked up. Pecos Bill swung his lariat and caught hold of the swirling funnel of air.

"Take good care of Widowmaker!" he shouted to Daniel.

"Don't go!" Daniel yelled back, but Pecos just waved.

"You can handle things on your own from now on!" he shouted, straddling the twister and waving his cowboy hat. "I'm a ring-tailed roarer! I can draw faster, shoot straighter, and ride harder than any man alive! *Yeeeeeeehaaaaaaw!"*

Daniel watched as Pecos dug in his spurs and rode the twister straight up into a thick mass of roiling storm clouds. Suddenly the clouds took on the shape of three figures, a burly logger wielding an ax, a railroad worker carrying a sledgehammer over his shoulder, and a cowboy twirling a lariat.

Daniel felt his eyes go misty with tears. "So long, Pecos," he called with a wave. Then he patted Widowmaker gently on the neck. "C'mon, boy, let's go home."

Widowmaker headed back to the farm, and Daniel rode him as proudly as any man could. He was Daniel's now, and together they would defend the Code. They would keep Paradise Valley just the way it was and never, ever spit in front of women or children.